Knockouts

A Northern Childhood

The Balaclava Story and other stories

Knockouts

General Editor: Josie Levine

Three Plays   Isobel D'Arcy
Mia   Gunnel Beckman
Mia Alone   Gunnel Beckman
The Marco File   Peter Buchanan
Save the Last Dance for Me and other stories   Jan Carew
Stranger than Tomorrow   Jan Carew
The Bike Racers   Bruce Carter
In the Beginning   John Christopher
The Six   Janet Green
The Six: Getting By   Janet Green
The Six: Turning Points   Janet Green
Rumble Fish   S E Hinton
Week Out   Geraldine Kaye
*A Northern Childhood: The Balaclava Story
    and other stories*   George Layton
A Northern Childhood: The Fib and other stories   George Layton
Long Journey Home   Julius Lester
The Job   Margaret Loxton
Odysseus Returns   Kenneth McLeish
The Robe of Blood and other stories   Kenneth McLeish
Ginger Mick   Joan Tate
Luke's Garden   Joan Tate
The Runners   Joan Tate
See You and other stories   Joan Tate
You Can't Explain Everything   Joan Tate
The Midwich Cuckoos   John Wyndham

Picture Story Books: *Cave Rescue, Danger at Sea,
    The Haunted Castle, Maiden Flight,
    Undersea Adventure*   Josie Levine

Cassette tapes, with readings of some of the stories, are available for
    the following:
The Marco File   read by Robert Powell
Save the Last Dance for Me   read by Valentine Dyall
Stranger than Tomorrow   read by Edward Petherbridge
The Six   read by Tony Robinson
The Six: Getting By   read by Michael Burlington and Anthony Hyde
The Six: Turning Points   ready by Brian Hewlett and David Goodland
*A Northern Childhood: The Balaclava Story
    and other stories*   read by George Layton
A Northern Childhood: The Fib and other stories
    read by George Layton
Long Journey Home   read by Guy Gregory and Valerie Murray
Odysseus Returns   read by Christian Rodska
The Robe of Blood   read by Jill Balcon
You Can't Explain Everything   read by Miriam Margolyes

Knockouts

A Northern Childhood

The Balaclava Story
and other stories

George Layton

Longman

Longman Group Limited
London
*Associated companies, branches and representatives
throughout the world*

For Tristan and Claudie

This edition first published by Longman Group 1975
Photographs by Lance Browne
Fourth impression 1980

ISBN 0 582 23345 3
Printed in Great Britain by
Hazell Watson & Viney Ltd, Aylesbury

Contents

The Balaclava story

The Balaclava story

Tony and Barry both had one. I reckon half the kids in our class had one. But I didn't. My mum wouldn't even listen to me.

'You're not having a balaclava! What do you want a balaclava for in the middle of summer?'

I must've told her about ten times why I wanted a balaclava.

'I want one so's I can join the Balaclava Boys . . .'

'Go and wash your hands for tea, and don't be so silly.'

She turned away from me to lay the table, so I put the curse of the middle finger on her. This was pointing both your middle fingers at somebody when they weren't looking – Tony had started it when Miss Taylor gave him a hundred lines for flicking paper pellets at

Jennifer Greenwood. He had to write out a hundred times:

'I must not fire missiles because it is dangerous and liable to cause damage to someone's eye.'

Tony tried to tell Miss Taylor that he hadn't fired a missile, he'd just flicked a paper pellet, but she threw a piece of chalk at him and told him to shut up.

'Don't just stand there – wash your hands.'

'Eh?'

'Don't say "eh", say "pardon".'

'What?'

'Just hurry up, and make sure the dirt comes off in the water, and not on the towel, do you hear?'

Ooh, my mum. She didn't half go on sometimes.

'I don't know what you get up to at school. How do you get so dirty?'

I knew exactly the kind of balaclava I wanted. One just like Tony's – a sort of yellowy-brown. His dad had given it to him 'cos of his ear-ache. Mind you, he didn't like wearing it at first. At school he'd give it to Barry to wear and got it back before home-time. But, all the other lads started asking if they could have a wear of it, so Tony took it back and said from then on nobody but him could wear it – not even Barry. Barry told him he wasn't bothered 'cos he was going to get a balaclava of his own – and so did some of the other lads – and that's how it started – the Balaclava Boys.

It wasn't a gang really. I mean they didn't have meetings or anything like that. They just went around together wearing their balaclavas, and if you didn't have one you couldn't go around with them. Tony and Barry were my best friends, but 'cos I didn't have a balaclava, they wouldn't let me go round with them. I tried.

'Aw, go on Barry, let us walk round with you.'

'No, you can't. You're not a Balaclava Boy.'

'Aw, go on.'

'No,'

'Please.'

I don't know why I wanted to walk round with them anyway. All they did was wander up and down the play-ground dressed in their rotten balaclavas. It was daft.

'Go on Barry, be a sport.'

'I've told you. You're not a Balaclava Boy. You've got to have a balaclava. If you get one, you can join.'

'But I can't, Barry. My mum won't let me have one.'

'Hard luck.'

'You're rotten.'

Then he went off with the others. I wasn't half fed-up. All my friends were in the Balaclava Boys. All the lads in my class except me. Wasn't fair. The bell went for the next lesson – ooh heck, handicraft with the Misery-guts Garnett – then it was home-time. All the Balaclava Boys were going in and I followed them.

'Hey Tony – do you want to go down the woods after school?'

'No – I'm going round with the Balaclava Boys.'

'Oh.'

Blooming Balaclava Boys. Why wouldn't *my mum* buy *me* a *balaclava*. Didn't she realise that I was losing all my friends – and just 'cos she wouldn't buy me one.

15

'Eh, Tony, we can go goose-gogging – you know by those super gooseberry bushes at the other end of the woods.'

'I've told you, I can't.'

'Yes, I know, but I thought you might want to go goose-gogging.'

'Well, I would – but I can't.'

I wondered if Barry would be going as well.

'Is Barry going round with the Balaclava Boys an' all?'

'Course he is.'

'Oh.'

Blooming balaclavas. I wish they'd never been invented.

'Why won't your mum get you one?'

'I don't know. She says it's daft wearing a balaclava in the middle of summer. She won't let me have one.'

'I found mine at home up in our attic.'

Tony unwrapped some chewing-gum and asked me if I wanted a piece.

'No thanks.' I'd've only had to wrap it in my handkerchief once we got in the classroom. You couldn't get away with anything with Mr Garnett.

'Hey, maybe you could find one in your

16

attic.'

For a minute I wasn't sure what he was talking about.

'Find what?'

'A balaclava.'

'No, we haven't even got an attic.'

I didn't half find handicraft class boring. All that mucking about with compasses and rulers. Or else it was weaving – and you got all tangled up with balls of wool. I was just no good at handicraft and Mr Garnett agreed with me. Today was worse than ever. We were painting pictures and we had to call it 'My favourite story'. Tony was painting *Noddy in Toyland*. I told him he'd get into trouble.

'Garnett'll do you.'

'Why – it's my favourite story.'

'Yes, but I don't think he'll believe you.'

Tony looked ever so hurt.

'But honest. It's my favourite story. Anyway what are you doing?'

He leaned over to have a look at my favourite story.

'Have you read it, Tony?'

'I don't know. What is it?'

'It's *Robinson Crusoe* – what do you think

it is?'

He just looked at my painting.

'Oh, I see it now. Oh yes, I get it now. I couldn't make it out for a minute. Oh yes, there's Man Friday behind him.'

'Get your finger off – it's still wet. And that isn't Man Friday, it's a coconut tree. And you've smudged it.'

We were using some stuff called poster paint, and I got covered in it. I was getting it everywhere, so I asked Mr Garnett if I could go for a wash. He gets annoyed when you ask to be excused, but he could see I'd got it all over my hands, so he said I could go, but told me to be quick.

The wash-basins were in the boys' cloak-room just outside the main hall. I got most of the paint off and as I was drying my hands that's when it happened. I don't know what came over me. As soon as I saw that balaclava lying there on the floor, I decided to pinch it. I couldn't help it. I just knew that this was my only chance. I've never pinched anything before – I don't think I have, but I didn't think of this as . . . well . . . I don't even like saying it – but . . . well stealing. I just did it.

I picked it up, went to my coat, and put it in the pocket. At least I tried to put it in the pocket but it bulged out, so I pushed it down the inside of the sleeve. My head was throbbing, and even though I'd just dried my hands, they were all wet from sweating. If only I'd thought a bit first. But it all happened so quickly. I went back to the classroom, and as I was going in I began to realise what I'd done. I'd *stolen* a balaclava. I didn't even know whose it was, but as I stood in the doorway I couldn't believe I'd done it. If only I could go back — in fact I thought I would but then Mr Garnett told me to hurry up and sit down. As I was going back to my desk I felt as if all the lads knew what I'd done. How could they? Maybe somebody had seen me. No! Yes! How *could* they? They could. Course they couldn't. No, course not. What if they did though? Oh heck.

I thought home-time would never come but when the bell did ring I got out as quick as I could. I was going to put the balaclava back before anybody noticed; but as I got to the cloakroom I heard Norbert Lightowler shout out that someone had pinched his balaclava. Nobody took much notice, thank goodness, and I heard Tony say to him that he'd most likely lost it. Norbert said he hadn't but he went off to make sure it wasn't in the classroom.

I tried to be all casual and took my coat, but I didn't dare put it on in case the balaclava popped out of the sleeve. I said tarah to Tony.

'Tarah Tony, see you tomorrow.'

'Yeh, tarah.'

Oh, it was good to get out in the open air. I couldn't wait to get home and get rid of that blooming balaclava. Why had I gone and done a stupid thing like that? Norbert Lightowler was sure to report it to the Headmaster, and there'd be an announcement about it at morning assembly and the culprit would be asked to own up. I was running home as fast as I could. I wanted to stop and take out the balaclava and chuck it away, but I didn't dare. The faster I ran, the faster my head was filled with thoughts. I could give it back to Norbert. You know, say I'd taken it by mistake. No, he'd never believe me. None of the lads would believe me. Everybody knew how much I wanted to be a Balaclava Boy. I'd have to get rid of the blooming thing as fast as I could.

My mum wasn't back from work when I got home, thank goodness, so as soon as I shut the front door, I put my hand down the sleeve of my coat for the balaclava. There was nothing there. That was funny, I was sure I'd put it down that sleeve. I tried down the other sleeve, and there was still nothing there. Maybe I'd got the wrong coat—no, it was my coat all right. Oh, blimey, I must've lost it while I was running home. I was glad in a way. I was going to have to get rid of it – now it was gone. I only hoped nobody had seen it drop out, but, oh, I was glad to be rid of it. Mind you, I was dreading going to school next morning. Norbert'll have probably reported it by now. Well, I wasn't going to own up. I didn't mind the cane – it wasn't that – but if you owned up, you had to go up on the stage in front of the whole school. Well I was going to forget about it now – and nobody would ever know that I'd pinched that blooming lousy balaclava.

I started to do my homework, but I couldn't concentrate. I kept thinking about assembly next morning. What if I went all red and everybody else noticed? They'd know I'd pinched it then. I tried to think about other things – nice things. I thought about bed. I just wanted to go to sleep. To go to bed and sleep. Then I thought about my mum. What she'd say if she knew I'd been stealing – but I still couldn't forget about assembly next day. I went into the kitchen and peeled some potatoes for my mum. She was ever so pleased when she came in from work and said I must've known she'd brought me a present.

'Oh, thanks. What've you got me?'

She gave me a paper bag and when I opened it I couldn't believe my eyes – a blooming balaclava.

'There you are, now you won't be left out and you can stop making my life a misery.'

'Thanks Mum.'

If only my mum knew she was making *my* life a misery. The balaclava she'd bought me was just like the one I'd pinched. I felt sick – I didn't want it. I couldn't wear it now. If I did, everybody would say it was Norbert Lightowler's. Even if they didn't, I just couldn't wear it. I wouldn't feel it was mine. I had to get rid of it. I went outside and put it down the lavatory. I had to pull the chain three times before it went away. It's a good job we've got an outside lavatory or else my mum would have wondered what was wrong with me.

I could hardly eat my tea.

'What's wrong with you? Aren't you hungry?'

'No, not much.'

'What've you been eating? You've been eating sweets haven't you?'

'No, I don't feel hungry.'

'Don't you feel well?'

'I'm alright.'

I wasn't, I felt terrible. I told my mum I was going upstairs to work on my model aeroplane.

'Well, it's my bingo night, so make yourself some cocoa before you go to bed.'

I went upstairs to bed, and after a while I fell asleep. The last thing I remember, was a big balaclava – with a smiling face – and it was the headmaster's face.

I was scared stiff when I went to school next morning. In assembly it seemed different. All the boys were looking at me. Norbert Lightowler pushed past and didn't say anything. When prayers finished I just stood there waiting for the Headmaster to ask for the culprit to own up – but he was talking about the school fete. And then he said he had something very important to announce – and I could feel myself going red. My ears were burning like anything and I was going hot and cold both at the same time.

'I'm very pleased to announce that the school football team has won the inter-league cup . . .'

And that was the end of assembly, except that we were told to go and play in the schoolyard until we were all called in, because there was a teachers' meeting. I couldn't understand why I hadn't been found out yet, but I still didn't feel any better – I'd probably be called to the headmaster's room later on.

I went out into the yard. Everybody was happy 'cos we were having extra playtime. I could see all the Balaclava Boys going round together – and then I saw Norbert Lightowler was one of them. I couldn't be sure it was Norbert 'cos he had a balaclava on, so I had to go up close to him. Yes, it was Norbert – he must have bought a new balaclava that morning.

24

'Have you bought a new one then, Norbert?'

'Y'what?'

'You've bought a new balaclava, have you?'

'What are you talking about?'

'Your balaclava. You've got a new bala-clava haven't you?'

'No, I never lost it, at all. Some fool had shoved it down the sleeve of my raincoat.'

The Christmas party

The Christmas party

Our classroom looked smashing. Lots of silver tinsel and crepe paper and lanterns. *We'd* made the lanterns, but Miss Taylor had bought the rest herself, out of her own money. Oh, only today and tomorrow and then we break up. Mind you, if school was like this all the time, I wouldn't be bothered about breaking up. Putting up Christmas decorations and playing games – much better than doing writing and spelling any day. I watched the snow coming down outside. Smashing! More sliding tomorrow. I love Christmas. I wish it was more than once a year. Miss Taylor started tapping on the blackboard with a piece of chalk. Everybody was talking and she kept on tapping 'till the only person you could hear was Norbert Lightowler.

'Look if I get a six and land on you, you

get knocked off and I still get another go!'

The whole class was looking at him.

'Look, when Colin got a six, he landed on *me* and *he* got another . . . !'

Suddenly he realised that he was the only one talking and he started going red.

'Thank you, Norbert, I think we all know the rules of Ludo.'

Miss Taylor can be right sarcastic sometimes. Everybody laughed. Even Miss Taylor smiled.

'Now, since it is getting so noisy, we're going to stop these games and do some work.'

Everybody groaned and Tony and me booed – quietly so Miss Taylor couldn't hear. She hates people that boo. She says people who boo are cowards.

'Who is that booing?'

We must have been booing louder than we thought.

'Who is that booing?'

Miss Taylor looked at Tony. I looked at Tony. They both looked at me. I put my hand up.

'It was me, Miss.'

Tony put his hand up.

'It was me an' all, Miss.'

She looked at us.

'You both know what I think of booing, don't you?'

We nodded.

'Yes, Miss.'

'Yes, Miss.'

'Don't ever let me hear it again.'

We shook our heads.

'No, Miss.'

'No, Miss.'

She turned to the class.

'Now, the work I have in mind is discussion work.'

Everybody groaned again – except me and Tony.

'I thought we'd discuss tomorrow's Christmas party!'

We all cheered and Miss Taylor smiled. We have a Christmas party every year, the whole school together in the main hall. Each class has its own table and we all bring the food from home.

'Now, does everybody know what they're bringing from home for the party tomorrow?'

I knew. I was bringing a jelly. I put my

hand up.

'I'm bringing a jelly, Miss!'

Everybody started shouting at once and Miss Taylor moved her hands about to calm us down.

'All right, all right, one at a time. Don't get excited. Jennifer Greenwood, what are you bringing?'

Jennifer Greenwood was sitting in the back row next to Valerie Burns. She wriggled her shoulders and rolled her head about and looked down. She always does that when she's asked a question. She's daft is Jennifer Greenwood.

'C'mon Jennifer, what are you bringing for tomorrow?'

She put her hand up.

'Please, Miss, I'm bringing a custard trifle, Miss.'

Norbert Lightowler pulled his mouth into a funny shape and pretended to be sick

'Ugh, I hate custard. I'm not gonna have any of that!'

Everybody laughed, except Miss Taylor.

'Well, Norbert – if I was Jennifer I wouldn't dream of giving you any. Right Jennifer?'

Jennifer just rolled her head about and giggled with Valerie Burns. Norbert was looking down at his desk.

'And Norbert, what are you bringing tomorrow?'

'Polony sandwiches, Miss, my mum's making 'em, and a bottle of mixed pickles, Miss, home-made!'

Miss Taylor said that would be lovely, and carried on asking right round the class. Tony said that he was bringing a Christmas cake. I was bringing the jelly that my mum was going to make, and Colin Wilkinson was bringing some currant buns. Valerie Burns said she was bringing some lemon-curd tarts, and Freda Holdsworth called her a spiteful cat 'cos *she* was bringing the lemon-curd tarts, and Valerie Burns *knew* she was bringing lemon-curd tarts 'cos she'd told her and she was a blooming copy-cat. Anyway Miss Taylor calmed her down by saying that it was a good job they were both bringing lemon-curd tarts, because then there would be enough for everybody, and everybody would want one, wouldn't they? And she asked everybody who would want a lemon-curd tart to put their hands up, and everybody put their hands up. Even I put my hand up and I hate lemon-curd. Well, it *was* Christmas.

After everybody had told Miss Taylor what they were bringing, she said that there'd be enough for the whole school, never mind just our class, but we should remember that Christmas isn't just for eating and parties, and she asked Tony what the most important thing about Christmas is.

'Presents, Miss!'

'No Tony, not presents. Christmas is when the baby Jesus was born, and that is the most important thing, and when you're all enjoying your presents and parties this year, you must all remember that. Will you all promise me?'

Everybody promised that they'd remember Jesus and then Miss Taylor started asking us all how we were going to spend Christmas. Freda Holdsworth said she was going to Bridlington on Christmas Eve to stay with her cousin, and on Christmas Eve they'd both put their stockings up for Father Christmas, but before they'd go to bed, they'd leave a glass of milk and some biscuits for him in case he's hungry. Norbert Lightowler said that that's daft 'cos there's no such thing as Father Christmas. Some of the others agreed, but most of 'em said course there is. I just wasn't sure. What I can't understand is, that if there *is* a Father Christmas, how does he get round everybody in one night? I mean the presents must come from somewhere, but how can he do it all by himself? And Norbert said how can there be only *one* Father Christmas, when he'd seen *two* down in town in Baldwin Street and another outside the fish market, and Neville Bastow said he'd seen one in Dickenson's (that's a big department store). Well, what about the one my mum had taken me to see at the Co-op. He'd promised to bring me a three-wheeler.

'Please Miss, there's one at the Co-op an' all. He's promised to bring me a three-wheeler.'

And then Miss Taylor explained that all these others are Father Christmas's brothers and relations who help him out 'cos he's so busy and Freda Holdsworth said Miss Taylor was right, and Norbert said he'd never thought of that, but that Paul Hopwood, he's in 2B, had told him that Father Christmas is just his dad dressed up, and I said that that's daft and

it couldn't be 'cos Father Christmas comes to
our house every year and I haven't got a dad,
and Miss Taylor said that if those who didn't
believe in Father Christmas didn't get any
presents, they'd only have themselves to blame,
and I agreed! Then she asked me what I'd be
doing on Christmas day.

'Well, Miss, when I wake up in the morning, I'll look round and see what presents I've
got, and I'll play with them and I'll empty my
stocking, and usually there are some sweets so
I'll eat them, and when I've played a bit more
I'll go and wake my mum up and show her
what I've got, and then I'll wake my Auntie
Doreen – she always stays with us every
Christmas; and then after breakfast I'll play
a bit more, and then we'll have us Christmas
dinner, and then we'll go to my grandad's and
I'll play a bit more there, and then I'll go home
to bed, and that'll be the end!'

Miss Taylor said that all sounded very nice
and she hoped everybody would have such a
nice Christmas, but she was surprised I wasn't
going to Church. Well, I told her that there
wouldn't really be time 'cos my grandad likes
us to be there early to hear Wilfred Pickles on

the wireless visiting a hospital, and to listen to The Queen talking, and then the bell went for home-time and Miss Taylor said we could all go quietly and told us not to forget our stuff for the party.

I went with Tony to get our coats from the cloakroom. Everybody was talking about the party and Barry was there shouting out that their class was going to have the best table 'cos their teacher had made them a Christmas pudding with money in it! I told him that was nothing 'cos Miss Taylor had given everybody in our class sixpence, but he didn't believe me.

'Gerraway, you bloomin' fibber.'

'She did, didn't she Tony?'

Tony shook his head.

'Did she heckers-like – she wouldn't give 'owt away.'

Huh! You'd think Tony'd've helped me kid Barry along.

'Well, she bought all our Christmas decorations for the classroom . . .' and I went to get my coat. I took my gloves out of my pocket and they were still soaking wet from snow-balling at playtime, so I thought I'd put them on the pipes to dry.

'Hey Tony, my gloves are still sodden.'

'Well put 'em on the pipes.'

'Yeh, that's a good idea.'

While they dried I sat on the pipes. Ooh, it was lovely and warm. There's a window above the basins and I could see the snow was still coming down – really thick now.

'Hey, it isn't half going to be deep to-morrow.'

Everybody had gone now except for Barry, Tony and me. Tony was standing on the basins looking out of the window and Barry was doing up his coat – it has a hood on it. I wish I had one like it. I could see through the door into the main hall where the Christmas tree was. It looked lovely. Ever so big. It was nearly up to the ceiling.

'Hey, isn't it a big Christmas tree?' Tony jumped down from the basin and came over to where I was sitting.

'Yeh. It's smashing. All them coloured balls. Isn't it lovely, eh Barry?'

Barry came over.

'Not bad. C'mon you two, let's get going, eh?'

'Just a sec', let's see if my gloves are dry.'

They weren't really but I put 'em on. As I was fastening my coat up Barry said how about going carol-singing to get a bit of money.

Tony was quite keen, but I didn't know. I mean my mum'd be expecting me home round about now . . .

'I suppose *you* can't come 'cos your mum'll be cross with you . . . as usual!'

Huh. It's all right for Barry. His mum and dad aren't bothered where he goes.

'Course I'll come. Where do you want to go?'

Barry said down near the woods where the posh live, but Tony said it was useless there 'cos they never gave you nowt. So we decided to go round Belgrave Road way, where it's only *quite* posh. It takes about ten minutes to get to Belgrave Road from our school and on the way we argued about which carols to sing. I wanted *Away in a Manger* but Barry wanted *O Come all Ye Faithful*.

'*Away in a Manger* isn't half as good as *O Come all Ye Faithful*, is it Tony?'

Tony shrugged his shoulders.

'I quite like *Once in Royal David's City*.'

In the end we decided to take it in turns to

37

choose. Belgrave Road's ever so long and we started at number three with *O Come all Ye Faithful*.

'O come all ye faithful, joyful and trium . . .'

That was as far as we got. A bloke opened the door, gave us three-halfpence and told us to push off.

Tony was disgusted.

'That's a good start, halfpenny each.'

Barry told him to stop grumbling.

'It's better than nothing. C'mon.'

We went on to number five and Tony and Barry started quarrelling again 'cos Tony said it was his turn to choose, but Barry wanted his go again 'cos we'd only sung one line. So we did *O Come all Ye Faithful* again.

'Oh come all ye faithful, joyful and triumphant,

Oh . . .'

We didn't get any further this time neither. An old lady opened the door and said her mother was poorly so could we sing a bit quieter. We started once more but she stopped us again and said it was still just a little bit too loud and could we sing it quieter.

'O come all ye faithful, joyful and triumphant,

O come ye, o come ye to Beth-eth-lehem . . .'

And we sang the whole thing like that, in whispers. We could hardly hear each other. I felt daft and started giggling and that set Tony and Barry off, but the old lady didn't seem to notice. She just stood there while we sang and when we finished she said thank you and gave us twopence each.

At the next house we sang *Once in Royal David's City* right through and then rang the doorbell – but nobody came. We missed number nine out 'cos it was empty and up for sale, and at number eleven we sang *Away in a Manger*.

We went right to the end of the road singing every carol we knew. We must've made about a pound between us by the time we got to the other end, and Barry said how about going back and doing the other side of the road. I was all for it, but I just happened to see St Chad's clock. Bloomin' heck! Twenty to nine! I couldn't believe it. I thought it'd be about half-past six, if that. Twenty to nine!

'Hey, I'd better get going. It's twenty to nine. My mum'll kill me!'

The other two said they were gonna do a

bit more carol-singing, so they gave me my share of the money and I ran home as fast as I could. I took a short cut through the snicket behind the fish and chip shop and I got home in about five minutes. I could see my Mum standing outside the front door talking to Mrs Theabould, our next door neighbour. She saw me and walked towards me. I tried to act all calm as if it was only about half-past five or six o'clock.

'Hullo Mum, I've been carol-singing.'

She gave me a clout. She nearly knocked me over. Right on my freezing cold ear an' all.

'Get inside, you! I've been going mad with worry. Do you know what time it is? Nine o'clock. Get inside!'

She pushed me inside and I heard her thank Mrs Theabould and come in after me. I thought she was gonna give me another clout, but she just shouted at me, saying that I was lucky she didn't get the police out, and why didn't I tell her where I was? By this time I was crying my head off.

'But I was only bloomin' carol-singing.'

'I'll give you carol-singing. Get off to bed,' and she pushed me upstairs into my bedroom.

'But what about my jelly for tomorrer. Have you made it?'

I thought she was going to go mad.

'Jelly! I'll give you jelly. If you think I've nothing better to do than make jellies while you're out roaming the streets! Get to bed!'

'But I've told Miss Taylor I'm bringing a jelly. I've got to have one. Please, Mum.'

She just told me to wash my hands and face and get to bed.

'And if I hear another word out of you, you'll get such a good hiding, you'll wish you hadn't come home ...' and she went downstairs.

I didn't dare say another word. What was I gonna do about my jelly? I had to bring one. I'd promised. There was only one thing for it. I'd have to make one myself. So I decided to wait 'till my mum went to bed, and then I'd go downstairs and make one. I don't know how I kept awake. I'm sure I nodded off once or twice, but after a while I heard my mum switch her light out, and when I'd given her enough time to get to sleep, I crept downstairs.

I've seen my mum make jellies tons of times and I knew you had to have boiling

water, so I put the kettle on. I looked in the
cupboard for a jelly and at first I thought I'd
had it, but I found one and emptied it into a
glass bowl. It was a funny jelly. Not like the
ones my mum usually has. It was sort of like
a powder. Still, it said jelly on the packet, so it
was all right. A new flavour most likely.
I poured the hot water into a bowl, closed the
cupboard door, switched off the light, and took
the jelly upstairs and I put it under my bed.
I could hear my mum snoring so I knew I was
all right, and I went to sleep.

Next thing I heard was my mum shouting
from downstairs.

'C'mon, get up or you'll be late for school.'

I got up and pulled the jelly from under the
bed. It had set lovely. All wobbly. But it was a
bit of a funny colour – sort of yellowy-white.
Still I'd got my jelly and that's what mattered.
My mum didn't say much when I got downstairs. She just told me to eat my breakfast and
get to school, so I did. When I finished I put
my coat on and said tarah to my mum in the
kitchen and went off. But first I sneaked upstairs and got my jelly and wrapped it in a
piece of newspaper.

The first thing we had to do at school was to take what we'd brought for the party into the main hall and stick on a label with our name on it and leave it on our table. Norbert Lightowler was there with his polony sandwiches and mixed pickles. So was Neville Bastow. Neville Bastow said that my jelly was a bit funny-looking, but Norbert said he loved jelly more than anything else, and he could eat all the jellies in the world. Miss Taylor came along then and told us to take our coats off and go to our classroom. The party wasn't starting till twelve o'clock, so in the morning we played games and sang carols and Miss Taylor read us a story.

Then we had a long playtime and we had a snowball fight with 2B, and I went on the slides 'till old Wilkie, that's the caretaker, came and put ashes on the ice. Then the bell went and we all had to go to our tables in the main hall. At every place was a Christmas cracker, and everybody had a streamer, but Mr Dyson, the headmaster, said that we couldn't throw any streamers until we'd finished eating. I pulled my cracker with Tony and got a red paper hat and a pencil sharpener. Tony got a blue hat and a small magnifying glass. When everybody had pulled their crackers we said grace and started eating. I started with a sausage roll that Neville Bastow had brought, and a polony sandwich.

Miss Taylor had shared my jelly out in bowls and Jennifer Greenwood said it looked horrible and wasn't going to have any. So did Freda Holdsworth. But Norbert was already on his jelly and said it was lovely and he'd eat anybody else's. Tony started his jelly and spat it out.

'Ugh, it's horrible.'

I tasted mine, and it *was* horrible, but I forced it down.

'It's not that bad.'

Just then Tony said he could see my mum.

'Isn't that your mum over there?'

He pointed to the door. She was talking to Miss Taylor and they both came over.

'Your mother says you forgot your jelly this morning, here it is.'

Miss Taylor put a lovely red jelly on the table. It had bananas and cream on it, and bits of orange. My mum asked me where I'd got my jelly from. I told her I'd made it. I thought she'd be cross, but she and Miss Taylor just laughed and told us to enjoy ourselves, and then my mum went off. Everybody put their hands up for a portion of my mum's jelly – except Norbert.

'I don't want any of that. This is lovely. What flavour is it?'

I told him it was a new flavour and I'd never heard of it before.

'Well, what's it called?'

'Aspic.'

'Y'what?'

'Aspic jelly – it's a new flavour!'

Norbert ate the whole thing and was sick afterwards, and everybody else had some of my mum's. It was a right good party.

The long walk

The long walk

I loved it when my Grandad took me out –
just me and him. I never knew when I was
going out with him. It just happened every so
often. My mum'd say to me, 'C'mon, get ready
'cos your grandad's coming to take you out.
Get your clogs on.' – and that was the one
thing that spoilt it – my clogs. Whenever my
grandad took me out, I had to wear a pair of
clogs that he'd given to me. Well he'd made
them you see, that was his job before he
retired, clog-maker. I didn't half make a noise
when I was wearing them an' all. Blimey you
could hear me a mile away. I hated those clogs.

'Aw, Mum, do I have to put my clogs on?'

'Now don't ask silly questions – go and get
ready.'

'Aw, please ask Grandad if I can go without
my clogs.'

'Do you want to go or don't you?'

My mum knew that I wanted to go.

'Course I want to go.'

'Then go and put your clogs on.'

'Oh, heck.'

Honest, I'd never ever seen anybody else wearing clogs. I wondered where my grandad would take me today. Last time I'd gone to the zoo with him – it was great. I was just about ready when I heard him knock at the front door. I knew it was my grandad, 'cos he always had his own special knock – everybody else used the bell. I could hear him downstairs – he was wearing clogs as well.

'I'm nearly ready, Grandad.'

I put on my windcheater that I'd been given last Christmas. It was maroon-coloured. My friend Tony had got one an' all only his was green, but I liked mine best – and I went downstairs.

'Hello, Grandad.'

My mum told me to give him a kiss.

'He's getting too big to give his old grandad a kiss, aren't you son?'

He always called me son.

'No, course not Grandad.'

He bent down so I could kiss him on his cheek. He was all bristly and it made me laugh.

'Ooh, Grandad, you haven't shaved today, have you?'

He was laughing as well. We were both laughing – we didn't really know why – and my mum started laughing. There we were, all three of us laughing at nothing at all .

'No son, I haven't shaved. But it doesn't matter today. It'll bother nobody else today. There's just the two of us.'

'Where are we going, Grandad, where are you taking us?'

He looked at me. His eyes were watering a bit and he wiped them with a dark blue hanky he always had in his top pocket.

'We're going on a walk – a special walk.'

He was almost whispering, as if he didn't want me mum to hear, bending down with his whiskery face next to mine.

'Where are we going, Grandad, where are we going? Is it a secret?'

'You'll see son, when we get there.'

He looked a bit sad for a minute, but then he smiled and put on his flat cap.

'C'mon son, let's get going.'

49

My mum gave us each a pack of sandwiches, and off we went. We must have looked a funny sight walking down the road together me and my grandad. Him dressed in his flat cap and thick overcoat and clogs. Me in my maroon windcheater and short grey trousers and clogs. But I was so happy. I didn't know where we were going and neither did anybody else. Only Grandad knew, and only I was going to find out.

'Are we walking all the way, Grandad?' He took such big strides that I was half walking and half running.

'No son, we'll get a trackless first to get out a bit.'

By 'trackless' he meant a bus, and I'd heard him say it so often that I never wondered why he said trackless.

'I'll show you where I used to go when I was a lad.'

We didn't have to wait long before a bus came, and we went upstairs and sat right at the front. Grandad was out of breath when we sat down.

'Are you all right, Grandad?'

'Oh, aye son. You get a better view up

here.'

'Yes, Grandad, you do.'

Soon we were going through the 'posh part' where the snobs lived. This was on the other side of the park.

'At one time there were no roof on't top deck. That were before the trackless. Completely open it was – daft really.'

The conductor came round for our fares.

'One and t'lad to the basin.'

I'd never heard of the basin before. After my grandad had paid our fares I asked him what it was.

'What's the basin, Grandad?'

'That's where we start our walk.'

'What basin is it? Why is it called "basin"?'

'The canal basin – it's where the canal starts. You'll see.'

By now we were going through a brand new shopping centre.

'Hey, look Grandad, that's where that new bowling alley is. My friends Tony and Barry have been. They say it's smashing.'

Grandad looked out of the window.

'That's where I used to play cricket – a long time ago.'

'Where the bowling alley is?'

'That's right son, when they were fields. It's all changed now. Mind, where we're going for our walk – it's not changed there. No, it's just the same there.'

We heard the conductor shout 'basin'.

'C'mon, son, our stop, be careful now. Follow me.'

While we were going down the stairs, I held tight onto my grandad. Not because I thought I might fall, but I was scared for him. He looked as though he was going to go straight from the top to the bottom.

"Are you alright, Grandad? Don't fall.'

He just told me not to be frightened and to hold on tight.

'That's right. You hold onto me son – you'll be all right – don't be frightened.'

We both got off the bus, and I watched it drive away. I didn't know where we were, but it was very quiet.

'It's nice here, isn't it Grandad?'

'This is where my dad was born – your great-grandad.'

It was a lovely place. There weren't many shops and there didn't seem to be many people either. By the bus stop was a big stone thing full of water.

'Hey, Grandad, is that where the horses used to drink?'

'That's right, son. I used to hold my grandad's horse there while it was drinking.'

I couldn't see anything like a basin.

I wondered where it was.

'Where's the basin, Grandad?'

'We've got to walk there. C'mon.'

We went away from the main street, into a side street, past all these little houses. I don't think any cars ever went down this street 'cos there was washing strung out right across the road – all the way down the street. Outside some of the houses were ladies washing down the front step and scraping that yellow stone on the edges. A lot of the houses had curtains over the front door, so that you could leave the door open and the wind didn't blow in. Mind you, it wasn't cold even though it was October. It was nice. The sun was shining – not hot – but just nice. When we got further down the street, I saw that it was a cul-de-sac.

'Hey, Grandad, it's a dead-end. We must've come the wrong way.'

Grandad just smiled.

'Do you think I'm that old, that I can't remember the way? Here, look.'

He took my hand and showed me the way. Just before the last house in the road was a tiny snicket. It was so narrow that we had to go through behind each other. I wouldn't have even noticed this snicket if my grandad hadn't shown it to me.

'Go on son, through there.'

It was very dark and all you could see was a little speck of light at the other end, so you can tell how long it was.

'You go first, Grandad.'

'No, after you, son.'

I didn't want to go first.

'No, you'd better go first, Grandad, 'cos you know the way, don't you.'

He laughed and put his hand in his pocket and brought out a few boiled sweets.

'Here you are. These are for the journey. Off we go for the last time.'

I was just going to ask him what he meant, but he carried on talking.

'I mean it'll soon be winter, won't it. Come on.'

And off we went through the dark passage. Grandad told me that when he was a kid they used to call it the Black Hole of Calcutta. Soon we reached the other end and it was quite strange 'cos it was like going through a door into the country. We ended up at the top of some steps – high up above the canal basin, and you could see for miles. I could only see one barge though, in the basin. We went down the steps. There were a hundred and fifteen steps – I counted them. Grandad was going down slowly so I was at the bottom before him.

'Grandad, there are a hundred and fifteen steps there, I counted them. C'mon let's look at that barge.'

I ran over to have a look at it and Grandad followed me.

'It's like a house isn't it, Grandad?'

'It is a house. Someone lives there. C'mon let's sit here and have our sandwiches.'

And we did.

The sun was very big and round, though it wasn't very hot, and the leaves on the trees were golden, and the reflection in the water made the canal look golden. There was nobody else about, and all the noises that you never noticed usually, suddenly sounded special, different. Like the siren that let the workers know it was dinner-time. I've heard sirens lots of times since then but they never sound so sweet. The same with the train. It must have been miles away 'cos I couldn't see any steam or anything, and you had to listen quite hard, but behind the hum of the country and town sounds mixed together, you could hear this knockety-knock.

When we'd finished our sandwiches we walked along the canal. Grandad showed me how to open the lock-gates, and we were both puffed out afterwards 'cos it was hard work. After a while we walked away from the canal, up a country lane. I don't suppose we were really that far away from home, but we seemed to be miles out in the country, and soon we came to a village. My grandad said we'd catch a bus home from there, but first he wanted to show me something, and he took hold of my hand. I didn't have a clue where he was taking me, but I got a shock when we ended up in the grave-yard. It had gone cold now. I wanted to go home.

'C'mon, Grandad, let's go home now.'

But he didn't seem to be listening properly.

'In a minute son, I just want to show you summat.'

And hand in hand we walked among the grave-stones.

'There you are, son, there's my plot. That's where I'll be laid to rest.'

I didn't know what to say.

'When, Grandad?'

'Soon'.

He smiled and looked very happy and he bent down and pulled out a couple of weeds. It was a very neat plot.

'C'mon son, we'd best get going now.'

When I told my mum that night that Grandad was going to die soon, she got very cross and told me not to talk like that.

'He's as fit as a fiddle is your grandad, Don't you talk like that.'

It happened three days later – at dinner-time. It came as a great shock to everybody, except of course to me and Grandad.

The holiday

The holiday

It wasn't fair. Tony and Barry were going. In fact, nearly all of them in Standard Three and Four were going – except me. It wasn't fair. Why wouldn't my mum let me go?

'I've told you – you're not going camping. You're far too young.'

Huh! She said that last year.

'You said that last year!'

'You can go next year when you're a bit older.'

She'd said that last year, too.

'You said that last year an' all.'

'Do you want a clout?'

'Well you did, Mum, didn't you?'

'Go and wash your hands for tea.'

'Aw, Mum, everybody else is going to school camp. Why can't I?'

Because you're coming to Bridlington with

me and your Auntie Doreen like you do every year.

"Cos you're coming to Bridlington with me and your Auntie Doreen like you do every year!'

I told you. Oh, every year the same thing, me mum, me, and me Auntie Doreen at Mrs Sharkey's boarding house. I suppose we'll have that room next door to the lavatory: a double bed for me mum and me Auntie Doreen, and me on a camp bed behind a screen.

'I suppose we'll have that rotten room again.'

'Don't be cheeky! Mrs Sharkey saves that room for me every year – last week in July and first week in August. It's the best room in the house, facing the sea like that, and nice and handy for the toilets. You know how important that is for your Auntie Doreen.'

'Aw, Mum, I never get any sleep – the sea splashing on one side and me Auntie Doreen on the . . . aw!'

Me mum gave me a great clout right across me head. She just caught me ear and all.

'Aw, bloomin' heck. What was that for?'

'You know very well. Now stop being so

cheeky and go and wash your hands.'

'Well, you've done it now. You've dislocated my jaw – that's it now. I'll report you to that RSPCC thing, and they'll sue you. You've really had it now . . . ow!'

She clouted me again – right in the same place.

'It's not fair. Tony's mum and dad are letting 'im go to school camp, and Barry's. Why won't you let me go?'

She suddenly bent down and put her face right next to mine, right close. She made me jump. Blimey, that moustache was getting longer. I wish she'd do something about it – it's embarrassing to have a mum with a moustache.

'Now, listen to me my lad. What Tony's mum and dad do, and what Barry's mum and dad do, is their lookout. You will come with me and your Auntie Doreen to Bridlington and enjoy yourself like you do every year!'

Huh! Enjoy myself – that's a laugh for a start. How can you enjoy yourself walking round Bridlington town centre all day looking at shops. You can do that at home. Or else, it was bingo. 'Key-of-the-door, old-age pension, legs-eleven, clickety-click' an' all that rubbish.

You could do that at home as well. And when we did get to the beach, I had to spend all day rubbing that oily sun stuff on me Auntie Doreen's back. It was horrible. Then the rain would come down and it was back to bingo. Honest, what's the point of going on holiday if you do everything that you can do at home? You want to do something different. Now camping, that's different. Tony's dad had bought him a special sleeping bag, just for going camping. Huh! I wish I had a dad.

'I bet if I had a dad, he'd let me go to school camp.'

I thought me mum was going to get her mad up when I said that, but she didn't at all.

'Go and wash your hands for tea, love. Your spam fritters will be ready in a minute.'

Ugh. Bloomin' spam fritters! Not worth washing your hands for!

'Yeh. All right.'

I started to go upstairs. Ooh, I was in a right mess now. I'd told all the other lads I was going. Our names had to be in by tomorrow. We had to give Mr Garnett our pound deposit. Well, I was going to go. I didn't care what me mum said, I was going to go – somehow!

When I got to the top of the stairs, I kicked a tin waste-paper bin on the landing. It fell right downstairs. It didn't half make a clatter.

'What on earth are you doing?'

She would have to hear, wouldn't she?

'Eh. It's all right, Mum. I just tripped over the waste-paper bin. It's all right.'

'Oh, stop playing the goat and come downstairs. Your tea's ready.'

What was she talking about, playing the goat? I couldn't help tripping over a waste-paper bin. Well, I couldn't have helped it if I had tripped over it, an' well, I might have done for all she knew. Well, I wasn't going to wash my hands just for spam fritters. Oh, bet we have macaroni cheese an' all. I went straight downstairs.

'Are your hands clean?'

'Yeh.'

'Here we are then. I've made some macaroni cheese as well.'

'Lovely.'

'C'mon. Eat it up quickly then we'll have a nice bit of telly.'

I didn't say anything else about the school camp that night. I knew it was no good. But

I was going to go. I'd told Tony and Barry I was going, I'd told all the lads I was going. Somehow, I'd get me own way. When I got to school next morning, I saw Tony and Barry with Norbert Lightowler over by the Black Hole. That's a tiny snicket, only open at one end, where we shove all the new lads on the first day of term. There's room for about twenty kids. We usually get about a hundred in. It's supposed to be good fun, but the new kids don't enjoy it very much. They get to enjoy it the next year.

'Hello, Tony. Hallo, Barry.'

Norbert Lightowler spat out some chewing gum. It just missed me.

'Oh, don't say "hello" to me then, will ya?'

'No. And watch where you're spitting your rotten chewing-gum – or you'll get thumped.'

Barry asked us all if we'd brought our pound deposit for school camp. Tony and Norbert had got theirs, of course. Nobody was stopping them going. I made out I'd forgotten mine.

'Oh heck. I must have left mine on the kitchen table.'

'Oh. I see. Well maybe Garnett'll let you

bring it tomorrow.'

I didn't say anything, but Norbert did.

'Oh, no. He said yesterday today's the last day. He said anybody not bringing their deposit today wouldn't be able to go. He did, you know.'

'Aw, shurrup, or I'll do you.'

'I'm only tellin' yer.'

'Well, don't bother.'

Tony asked me if I'd learnt that poem for Miss Taylor. I didn't know what he was talking about.

'What poem?'

Norbert knew of course. He brought a book out of his pocket.

'*Drake's Drum*. Haven't you learnt it?'

Oh crikey! *Drake's Drum*. With all this worry about trying to get to school camp, I'd forgotten all about it. Miss Taylor had told us to learn it for this morning.

'We're supposed to know it this morning, you know.'

'I know, Norbert, I know.'

Honest, Norbert just loved to see you in a mess, I suppose 'cos he's usually in trouble himself.

'*I* know it. I spent all last night learning it.
Listen:

"Drake he's in his hammock an' a
thousand mile away.
Captain, art thou sleeping there below?
Slung a' tween the round shot in
Nombres Dios bay . . .".'

I snatched the book out of his hands.

'Come 'ere. Let's have a look at it.'

'You'll never learn it in time. Bell'll be
going in a minute.'

'You were reading it, anyway.'

'I was not. It took me all last night to learn
that.'

Barry laughed at him.

'What all last night to learn three lines?'

'No, clever clogs. I mean the whole poem.'

Just then, the bell started going for
assembly. Norbert snatched his book back.

'C'mon, we'd better get into line. Garnett's
on playground duty.'

Norbert went over to where our class was
lining up. Barry's in Standard Four, so he
went over to their column.

'See you at playtime.'

'Yeh. Tarah.'

While we were lining up, we were all talking. Mr Garnett just stood there with his hands on his hips, staring at us, waiting for us to stop.

'Thank you,'

Some of us heard his voice and stopped talking. Those that didn't carried on.

'Thank you.'

A few more stopped, and then a few more, till the only voice you could hear was Norbert Lightowler's, and as soon as he realised nobody else was talking, he shut up quick.

'Thank you. If I have to wait for silence as long as that at the end of this morning's break, then we shall spend the whole break this afternoon learning how to file up in silence. Do you understand?'

We all just stood there, hardly daring to breathe.

'Am I talking to myself? Do you understand?'

Everybody mumbled 'Yes, Sir', except Norbert Lightowler. He had to turn round and start talking to me and Tony.

'Huh! If he thinks I'm going to spend my playtime filing up in silence, he's got another think coming.'

'Lightowler!'

Norbert nearly jumped out of his skin.

'Are you talking to those boys behind you?'

'No, Sir. I was just telling 'em summat . . .'

'Really?'

'Yes, Sir . . . er . . . I was just . . . er . . . telling them that we have to give our pound in today, Sir, for school camp, Sir.'

'I want a hundred lines by tomorrow morning: "I must not talk whilst waiting to go into assembly".'

'Aw, Sir.'

'Two hundred.'

He nearly did it again, but stopped just in time, or he'd 've got three hundred.

'Right. When I give the word, I want you to go quietly into assembly. And no talking. Right – wait for it. Walk!'

Everybody walked in not daring to say a word. When we got into the main hall, I asked Tony for the book with *Drake's Drum* in, and during assembly, I tried to snatch a look at the poem but, of course, it was a waste of time. Anyway, I was more worried about my pound deposit for Mr Garnett. After prayers, the headmaster made an announcement about it.

'This concerns only the boys in Standards
Three and Four. Today is the final day for
handing in your school camp deposits. Those
of you not in 3B must see Mr Garnett during
morning break. Those of you in 3B will be
able to hand in your money when Mr Garnett
takes you after Miss Taylor's class. Right,
School turn to the right. From the front
Dismiss! No talking.'

I had another look at the poem while we
were waiting for our turn to go.

> "Drake he's in his hammock and a
>   thousand mile away,
> Captain, art thou sleeping there
>   below?"

Well, I knew the first two lines. Tony wasn't
too bothered. He probably knew it.

'Don't worry. She can't ask everybody to
recite it. Most likely she'll ask one of the girls.
Anyway, what are you going to do about
Garnett? Do you think he'll let you bring your
pound deposit tomorrow?'

'Yeh, sure to.'

If only Tony knew that it'd be just as bad
tomorrow. I had to get a pound from somewhere. Then I'd have about four weeks to get
my mum to let me go. But I had to get me

name down today or I'd . . . I'd had it. Miss Taylor was already waiting for us when we got into our classroom.

'Come along children. Settle down.'

Miss Taylor took us for English and Religious Instruction.

'Now today, we're going to deal with some parts of the Old Testament.'

Tony and me looked at each other. She'd got mixed up. Today was English and tomorrow was Religious Instruction.

'Now you've all heard of the Ten Commandments . . .'

Bloomin' hummer. What a let-off. Tony was grinning at me.

'Do any of you know the first of these Ten Commandments?'

Jennifer Greenwood put her hand up. She was the top of the class every year. Everyone reckoned she was Miss Taylor's favourite.

'Yes, Jennifer.'

Jennifer Greenwood wriggled about a bit in her seat and went red. She's always going red.

'Please, Miss, it's English this morning, Miss; it's Religious Instruction tomorrow, Miss.'

Honest, I could've thumped her. Then Norbert put his hand up.

'Yes, Miss. You told us to learn *Drake's Drum* for this morning, Miss.'

I leaned across to Tony.

'I'll do him at playtime.'

'Quite right, Norbert. Thank you for reminding me. Now, who will recite it for me?

Everybody shoved their hands up shouting, 'Miss, Miss, me Miss, Miss', so I thought I'd better look as keen as the rest of them.

'Miss! Miss! Miss!'

I stretched my hand up high. I got a bit carried away. I was sure she'd pick one of the girls.

'Me, Miss. Please, Miss. Me, Miss!'

She only went and pointed at me. I couldn't believe it.

'Me, Miss?'

'Yes. You seem very keen for once. Stand up and speak clearly.'

I stood up as slowly as I could. My chair scraped on the floor and made a noise like chalk on the blackboard.

'Hurry up, and lift your chair up. Don't push it like that.'

Everybody was lookin' at me. Norbert who

sits in the front row had turned round and was grinning.

'Er . . . um *Drake's Drum* . . . by Henry Newbolt . . .'

Miss Taylor lifted up her finger.

'*Sir* Henry Newbolt!'

'Yes, Miss.'

I was glad she stopped me. Anything to give me more time.

'Carry on.'

I took a deep breath. I could feel Norbert still grinning at me.

'Ahem. *Drake's Drum* . . . by Sir Henry Newbolt.'

I stopped: then I took another deep breath . . .

"Drake is in his cabin and a thousand mile away . . ."

I stopped again. I knew after the next line, I'd be in trouble.

"Cap'n, art thou sleeping down below. . ."

The whole class was listening. I didn't know what I was going to say next. I took another breath and I was just about to tell Miss Taylor I couldn't remember any more, when Norbert burst out laughing. Miss Taylor went over to him:

'What are you laughing at, Norbert?'

'Nothing, Miss.'

'You think you can do better – is that it?'

'No, Miss.'

'Stand up!'

Norbert stood up. Miss Taylor looked at me. 'Well done. That was a very dramatic opening. Sit down, and we'll see if Norbert Lightowler can do as well.'

I couldn't believe it. Tony could hardly keep his face straight.

Norbert went right through the poem. Miss Taylor had to help him once or twice, but he just about got through. Miss Taylor told him he hadn't done badly, but not quite as well as me. After that a few of the others recited it, and then we went on to do some English grammar.

After Miss Taylor, we had Mr Garnett. He gave the girls some arithmetic to do, while he sorted out the deposits for school-camp. He went through the register, and everybody that was going gave him their pound deposit – till he got to me.

'I've forgotten it, Sir.'

'You know today is the last day, don't you?'

'Yes, Sir.'

'And all the names have to be in this morning? I told you all that yesterday, didn't I?'

'Yes, Sir. Yes, Sir – I'll bring me pound tomorrow, Sir.'

Mr Garnett tapped his pencil.

'I'll put the pound in for you, and I want you to repay me first thing tomorrow morning. All right?'

'Er . . . um . . . yes, Sir. I think so, Sir.'

'You do want to go to school camp?'

'Yes, Sir.'

'Right then. Don't forget to give me your pound tomorrow.'

'No, Sir.'

I didn't know what I was going to do now. I reckoned the best thing was to tell Mr Garnett the truth, so when the bell went for playtime, I stayed behind in the classroom, and I told him about me mum wanting me to go to Bridlington with her and me Auntie Doreen. He told me not to worry, and gave me a letter to give to me mum that night. I don't know what it said, but after me mum had read it, she put it in her pocket and said she'd give me a pound for Mr Garnett in the morning.

'Can I go to camp, then?'

'Yes, if that's what you want.'

'I don't mind coming to Bridlington with you and Auntie Doreen, if you'd rather.' ..

Me mum just got hold of me face with both her hands.

'No, love, you go to school camp and enjoy yourself.'

So I did – go to school camp, that is – but I didn't enjoy myself. It was horrible. They put me in a tent with Gordon Barraclough: he's a right bully and he gets everybody on to his side 'cos they're all scared of him. I wanted to go in Tony and Barry's tent, but Mr Garnett said it would upset all his schedules, so I was stuck with Gordon Barraclough and his gang. They made me sleep right next to the opening so when it rained, my sleeping-bag got soaked. And they thought it was dead funny to pull me clothes out of me suitcase (me mum couldn't afford a rucksack) and throw them all over the place.

'Huh! Fancy going camping with a suit-case!'

'Mind your own business, Barraclough! Me mum couldn't afford a proper rucksack. Anyway, I'm off to Bridlington on Sunday.'

And I meant it. Sunday was parents visiting day, and me mum and Auntie Doreen were coming to see me on their way to Bridlington. So I was going to pack up all my stuff and go with them. Huh ... I couldn't stand another week with Gordon Barraclough. I wish I'd never come.

So on Sunday morning after breakfast in the big marquee, I packed everything into me suitcase and waited for me mum and me Auntie Doreen to come. They arrived at quarter to eleven.

'Hello, love. Well, isn't it grand here. You are having a nice time, aren't you?'

'Yeh, it's not bad, but I want to tell you summat.'

Me mum wasn't listening. She was looking round the camp site.

'Well, it's all bigger than I thought. Is this your tent here?'

She poked her 'ead through the flap. I could hear her talking to Gordon Barraclough and the others.

'No! No! No! Don't move boys. Well, haven't you got a lot of room in here? It's quite deceiving from the outside.'

Her head came out again.

76

'Here, Doreen, you have a look in here. It's ever so roomy.'

She turned back to Gordon Barraclough.

'Well, bye-bye boys. Enjoy the rest of your holiday. And thank you for keeping an eye on my little lad.'

I could hear them all laughing inside the tent. I felt sick.

'Mum, I want to ask you something.'

'In a minute love, in a minute. Let's just see round the camp, and then we'll have a little natter before your Auntie Doreen and me go. Oh, and I want to say hello to Mr Garnett while I'm here. You know, on the way here today, I kept saying wouldn't it be lovely if I could take you on to Bridlington with us. Wasn't I, Doreen? But now I'm here, I can see you're all having a real good time together. You were right, love, it's much better to be with your friends than with two fuddy-duddies like us, eh, Doreen? Well, c'mon love, aren't you going to show us round? We've got to get our bus for Bridlington soon.'

I showed them both round the camp-site, and they went off just before dinner. I didn't feel like anything to eat myself. I just went to the tent and unpacked me suitcase.

The gang-hut

The gang-hut

We used to have a gang-hut – Barry, Tony, and me. It was smashing. It used to be in Tony's back garden – in fact I think it's still there. I remember one of the last meetings we ever had – it weren't long after August Bank Holiday. I went to the gang-hut straight after school. There were a short-cut you could take over a broken wall – you got a bit mucky, but it were quicker. I got to the hut and knocked the secret knock, two quick knocks – a pause – then followed by three more.

'Give the password'.

That was Barry – he was our leader. I stared at the door which had 'The Silent Three' painted on it (I'd done that), and thought.

'What password?'

'What do you mean – what password?'

'What do *you* mean – what do I mean –

what password?'

Barry's voice suddenly became deeper, and rather bossy!

'Well, if you'd attended the last gang meeting, you would have known what password!'

Oh, course, that's why I didn't know this blooming password that Barry was talking about. Course, I didn't go to the last gang meeting. How can you go on Bank Holiday Monday? I'd gone with me mum and Auntie Doreen to Scarborough – aye, and it rained all blooming day. I'd felt a bit daft carrying my bucket and spade and ship on the sea front when it was pouring with rain. Yes, and when I'd cheeked my Auntie Doreen off my mum had hit me, and I'd cried – even though it didn't hurt.

'Come on, Barry – tell us what the password is.'

'Well, you haven't to tell anybody.'

'Course not.'

'All right then – it's "Ouvrez la porte".'

'Y'what.'

' "Ouvrez la porte".'

I didn't know what he were talking about.

'It's a blooming long password, isn't it?'

'It's three words – they're French. Not many people will know what it means.'

'What does it mean?'

'It means "open the door".'

'It's a bit ordinary, isn't it?'

'Not if you say it in French.'

'Yes, I suppose so. Anyway, open the door.'

'Say the password!'

'You know it's me – let us in!'

'Say the password!'

'Oh, all right – "Ouvrez la porte".'

At last I was in the den. It was only small – but at least it was ours – Barry's, Tony's and mine – that is – 'The Silent Three' – and now that we'd got a lock and key from Barry's dad, nobody else could get in. Come to think of it, neither could me and Tony, 'cos Barry always kept the key, seeing as his Dad had given us the lock. Tony had said that *he* should keep they key 'cos the den was in his back garden. I'd agreed – not that I wanted Tony to have the key either, but Barry always got things his way – he used to be like that a lot, Barry did, pushing his weight around and telling us how much better he did things than we did. Barry started going on about Tony being late.

'Where's Tony, isn't he coming?'

Tony was in the same class as me.

'Yes, but Miss Taylor kept him in for eating in class. Rotten thing. She's always keeping people in, y'know.'

'Yes, I know. She took us last year.'

Barry was in Standard Four and was going in for his scholarship in December. Tony and me were only in Standard Three. If I'd been taking my scholarship, I'd have been scared stiff, but Barry didn't seem to be.

'Eh, Barry, do you think you'll be scared when you take your scholarship?'

'Yeh, course, everybody gets scared. Wouldn't you?'

'Oh, yeh, I know everybody gets scared, but I just wondered if you did. Which grammar school do you want to go to if you pass?'

'Oh, I don't know – same as my brother I suppose – I don't know.'

Just then, there were two knocks on the door, followed by three more.

'Hey Barry, that might be Tony.'

'What do you mean, might be Tony – it must be Tony – he's the only other one who knows the secret knock, isn't he?'

'Oh, yeh – eh, ask him the password – go on – ask him!'

'I'm going to, don't you worry. Give the password!'

I heard Tony's voice stuttering, trying to think of the password. Oh, ho, he'd forgotten it. He didn't know it. I was right glad he didn't know it.

'Do you know it? Do you know it? You can't come in if you don't know it, can he, Barry?'

'Hang on, I'm thinking. I'll get it, don't tell me. Err . . . I know! "Ouv the report".'

'No, "ouvrez la porte".'

'Well, near enough, wasn't it, let us in.'

'All right, come on.' Barry opened the door and let Tony in.

'Now we all know the password, don't we.'

I knew Barry would say something.

'You should have known it before. I shouldn't really have let you in.'

'Well, I nearly knew it, didn't I, Barry?'

Tony looked at Barry for some kind of praise. Although Tony and me didn't really like Barry being the leader of 'The Silent

Three', we accepted him as such, and also accepted his decisions on certain gang matters. It was Barry, for instance, who had decided on the gang's policy, which was 'to rob the rich to help the poor', 'cos that was what Robin Hood did – although it was Tony who had thought of the name 'The Silent Three'.

We had lots of things in the gang-hut. There was a window, with a frame which opened and closed on proper hinges. You had to admire Barry 'cos he'd made that – it was very clever. Of course, there was no real glass in it, but there was some sacking which kept nosy parkers out. There was also a picture on one of the stone walls – it showed a lady, dressed in a long white robe, holding a little baby on her knee – and the baby had long curly hair and it didn't have any clothes on – but you couldn't tell if it was a boy or a girl. *Barry* didn't like it 'cos he thought it looked soppy. Tony said his grandma had given it to him, and that they ought to be glad they had it 'cos he bet there weren't many gangs that had a picture. I thought it looked nice.

There was also a table, which had two drawers – one for Barry, and one for me and

Tony to share. We kept all sorts of things in it
– from a rubber stamp which said 'Albert
Holdsworth (Worsteds) Limited' to half a
potato which, when you dipped it into some
paint, and stamped it, said 'The Silent Three'.
We had one chair, and we took it in turns to
sit in it, and two orange boxes. Also, there was
a small carpet which my mum was going to
throw away. She'd said to me – 'Oh, you don't
want that dirty old thing'. And I'd said yes,
I did – and I'd muttered something about the
fight against evil and 'The Curse of the Silent
Three', but by then my mum wasn't listening.
Anyway the most important thing was that
I'd got the carpet and proudly presented it to
Barry and Tony at the next gang meeting, and
what had really pleased me was that the other
two were impressed as I'd hoped they'd be.
Well, that was really all we had in the gang-
hut, oh, except two candles which were kept
for emergency.

'What shall we do then?'

Tony looked at Barry for an answer. This
was usually the way gang meetings started, and
most times the question was directed towards
Barry, 'cos his were usually the best ideas, and

anyway, we always did what he suggested.

'Well, first I've got to give you the secret seal – the curse of "The Silent Three".'

I knew this was what Barry would say, and it was just what I didn't want.

'Oh, not again, Barry. I got into trouble with my mum last time. It took ages to get it off. My mum says I haven't to let you do it again.'

This didn't bother Barry.

'You've got to have the Secret Seal or else you're not a member of "The Silent Three" – isn't that right, Tony?'

Tony had to agree, although I knew by his face, *he* wasn't that keen to have the stamp *either*.

'Anyway, it won't go on so strong this time, 'cos I won't put any more paint on.'

Barry took out the half potato from his drawer. It had dried blue paint on it from the last time we'd used it, and he spat on it to make it wet.

'Ooh, we'll all get diseases!'

'No, you won't. Hold out your hand.'

'No, I'm not having your spit all over me.'

'C'mon, you've got to have it or you'll be

banned from 'The Silent Three'. You've got to have it, hasn't he, Tony?'

Tony nodded in agreement, but he was even more reluctant now than he was earlier on. Barry looked right at me.

'C'mon – are you going to have it or not?'

I just sat there.

'Well, you should have let us do our own spitting.'

'Well, it's too late now. Are you going to have it or not?'

'No, I'm not!'

Barry just lost his temper then and threw the potato on the floor.

'Well, I'm not bothered about the secret seal anyway – or the gang-hut for that matter. I was only joining in to please you kids!'

Tony and me, he meant. I was really shocked – 'cos I mean after all he was the leader of 'The Silent Three'. I didn't know what to say. I just sat there.

Tony picked up the potato, I held my hand out and he stamped it – then he stamped his own. He tried to stamp Barry's hand, but Barry wouldn't let him. 'The Silent Three' sat in silence – me and Tony waiting for the secret

seal to dry and Barry – well – just not inter-
ested.

When the secret seal had dried, I started to
talk to Barry.

'Eh, Barry, you know that kid in your class
with that big red patch on his face . . .'

'That's a birthmark!'

'Yer, that big red birthmark. He was crying
his head off in the lavatory this morning.'

'Yeh, I know, his grandad died last night.
He went home at dinner time.'

'I remember my grandad. We used to go
for walks when I was little. He's dead now.
I don't remember my grandma though. She
died when I was two.'

'What about your other grandad and
grandma?'

I didn't know what Barry was talking
about. I looked at him.

'What other grandad and grandma?'

'Your other grandad and grandma. You
know your other grandad and grandma. You
have two grandads and grandmas, you know.
Oh, don't you even know that.'

Tony said that he had two an' all.

'Yes, I've got two grandads and grandmas.

I've got my grandad and my grandma Atkinson, and my grandad and my grandma Spencer.'

Barry seemed to be really enjoying this.

'Oh, don't you know you have two grandads and grandmas?'

'All I know is, I've never seen my grandma, 'cos she died when I was two, and my grandad's dead an' all.'

And as far as I was concerned, that was that, although really it surprised me to hear that Barry and Tony both had two sets of grandads and grandmas. Why hadn't I – I'd have to ask me mum.

Tony and Barry started talking about swimming.

'We start swimming lessons next year.'

Tony meant me and him. You didn't have swimming lessons until you got into Standard Four. Barry had been having lessons for a while – he was quite good.

'I can do two lengths, and a half a length on my back.'

Tony could float a bit.

'I'm right looking forward to having swimming lessons, aren't you?'

I wasn't really looking forward to having swimming lessons. To be quite honest, I was scared stiff.

'Yes, I suppose so. I might be a bit scared though.'

'What for?' Oh, it was all right for Barry to talk.

'What is there to be scared about. You scared you might drown?'

Yes, I was.

'Course I'm not.'

I'd only been to the swimming baths once in my life, and somebody had pushed me in then. It was very scaring – I thought I was going to drown that time. The pool attendant had pulled me out and thumped the lad who'd pushed me in. I'd never been to the baths again since then. Barry was still going on about being scared.

'There's nowt to be scared of, y'know. It's dead easy, swimming is. Isn't it, Tony?'

'I don't know, I can't swim. I can float a bit.'

'Ah, floating's easy – anyone can float.'

Huh, I couldn't! I was fed up with this talk about swimming. It reminded me too much of what was to come. So I started to talk about something else.

'Eh, it'll be bonfire night soon.'

This got us all quite excited and Barry said we'd have the biggest bonfire in the neighbourhood. Tony said we should start collecting wood 'cos it was the end of August already.

'We'll have to go down the woods – we could go down on Sunday afternoon.'

Barry agreed, but I said I'd have to ask my mum.

'You're always having to ask her. Can't you do anything without asking her?'

'Course I can, but she doesn't like me going down those woods.'

I had to go then 'cos my mum told me I had to be in by a quarter to six. Tony had to go too, 'cos he was sleeping at our house that weekend, 'cos his mum was going away to stay with his big sister for a few days, who was married and lived in Manchester.

'My mum says by the time she gets back from Manchester, I'll be an uncle.'

So the gang meeting ended. Tony and me had to go to town next day with my mum, but we said we'd see Barry at the gang-hut at about four o'clock. Barry said all right, and that he was going home to see if he could find any empty bottles to take back to the shop so he'd have some money to buy toffees for the Saturday morning matinee.

Barry started locking up the hut.

'Eh, are you two going to the pictures tomorrow morning?'

'I don't know. We might do. See you tomorrow afternoon anyway. Tarah.'

I asked my mum that night why I didn't have two grandads and grandmas like Tony and Barry, but she just told me not to ask silly questions and to get on with my supper.

We didn't go to the matinee next day 'cos my mum said that we both had to have our hair cut before going into town that afternoon. I tried to get out of it, but I couldn't, and Tony didn't help either 'cos he agreed with my mum and said we did really need our hair cut.

Anyway that was what happened, and at about quarter to four, we came back from town with lots of shopping. Tony and me changed out of our best suits – mine was brand new – I only got it just before t'Bank Holiday – and we went straight over to the gang-hut. Well, we just got over the broken wall into Tony's backyard, and I knew something was wrong – and when I realised what it was I just couldn't believe it; the whole gang-hut was wrecked. Honest, I'll never forget it. The door was wide open and inside the place was in a real mess – the two orange boxes were broken, the table was knocked over, the picture (of the lady) was lying on the floor. The window frame was pulled away from the hinges.

It was awful. All I could feel was this great thumping in my head.

'Hey, Tony, I wonder who did it?'

'Barry did. Look!'

He pointed to the door, and instead of 'The Silent Three', it said 'The Silent Two'.

'Why did he do it?'

Tony shrugged his shoulders and said he'd probably felt like it.

Neither of us knew then why Barry had done it, but Tony somehow didn't seem too bothered neither. I suppose he knew that he'd be the leader of the gang now. *I* just couldn't understand it at all – why would Barry wreck the whole gang-hut like this, especially since he had built most of it himself – specially the window frame.

When Tony left the gang, I became leader – for a while – Tony didn't do anything like wrecking the hut, nor did I when I left – we just got tired of it and – well . . . lost interest.

Some other younger lads used the hut for their meetings after us, but Barry, Tony and me weren't bothered. We didn't care who had the gang-hut now.